Margo Thinks Twice

To my mother, for worrying about us

Margo Thinks Twice

Written and illustrated by MONICA ARNALDO

OWLKIDS BOOKS

Margo woke up early one Saturday with an urge to create. She crept around the house collecting everything she needed. Just as she began to glue—a very important step according to Margo—her mother appeared in the doorway.

"Easy with the glue, Margo!"
her mother said.

"But I'm making something!"
said Margo.

"Well, be careful," her mother laughed as she continued down the hall. "The last thing we need is you sticking to everything."

Margo hadn't considered this...

Margo spent the afternoon outside, far from the worrisome glue pot. She was about to leap from her swing when she heard her mother calling.

"Keep that bottom planted, Margo!"

"But I'm about to break the world record!" said Margo.

"Well, be careful. It's getting windy, and there's no telling where you'll land."

It was true that Margo hadn't factored in the wind...

Later that day, Margo's mother announced they had errands to run. When the pair entered the clothing store, Margo brightened and ducked straight into the racks of clothes.

"Time to come out, Margo!" her mother said as she headed to the checkout.

"But I'm playing jungle explorers!" said Margo.

"Well, be careful. We don't want you getting lost on your adventure."

Margo's hamster, Poppy, had gotten lost last year while she was giving him a tour of the house. The family had never seen him again. Margo imagined being lost like Poppy and began to worry in earnest.

Margo gripped her mother's hand
tightly as they left the store.

"Just one last stop," said Margo's mother.
"Let's see what kinds of critters they
have in here..."

"Okay, but let's be careful…"
whispered Margo.

"Margo, look!" her mother said.

Margo peeked. They had reached the back of the shop and stopped in front of a gate.

A creature padded toward her...

It was a hungry wolf!

It was a big brown bear!!

It was a terrifying—

A big, sloppy kiss landed on Margo's face.
She looked into the creature's eyes and saw a friendly
dog smiling back at her!

Margo peered around the shop. The loud
squawks were coming from a tiny bird.
The giant prickly creature had deflated into
a thin little fish.

"What do you think?" Margo's mother asked. "Should we take him home?"

"Well, he might get into all sorts of trouble. And he might be clumsy. And messy. And…"

"Just like us?" her mother said gently.

This time, Margo didn't have to think twice.

"He'll fit right in!" she laughed, wrapping their new dog in a great big hug.